G.I. JOE
A Real A[...]™

ANTI-VENOM

by Michael Anthony Steele
Illustrated by The Thompson Brothers

SCHOLASTIC INC.

New York   Toronto   London   Auckland   Sydney
Mexico City   New Delhi   Hong Kong   Buenos Aires

No part of this publication may be reproduced in whole or in part, or stored in
a retrieval system, or transmitted in any form or by any means, electronic,
mechanical, photocopying, recording, or otherwise, without written permission
of the publisher. For information regarding permission, write to Scholastic Inc.,
Attention: Permissions Department, 557 Broadway, New York, NY 10012.

ISBN 0-439-62688-9

HASBRO and its logo, G.I. JOE, and all related characters
are trademarks of Hasbro, and are used with permission.
© 2004 Hasbro. All Rights Reserved.

Published by Scholastic Inc.
SCHOLASTIC and associated logos are trademarks
and/or registered trademarks of Scholastic Inc.

Interior design by Rocco Melillo

12 11 10 9 8 7 6 5 4 3 2 1   4 5 6 7 8 9/0

Printed in the U.S.A.
First printing, September 2004

CHAPTER 1

"Hang on!" Duke shouted over the roar of the helicopter blades. "You're almost safe!"

A frightened man dangled over the roof of his house. The helicopter's winch slowly reeled in the cable that held him. Heavy Duty piloted the Night Attack Chopper while Duke pulled the man aboard. He was the last person rescued from the flooded town.

"Thank you very much," said the man. Duke wrapped a blanket around him and buckled him in his seat. "I don't know what happened. One minute, everything was fine. The next minute, the whole town is flooded and I'm trapped on my roof."

"Don't worry," said Duke. "We'll get to the bottom of this."

They dropped the man off at a shelter and then flew to the local dam. The water behind the dam was dangerously high. High Tech and Snake Eyes were waiting for them on one bank.

"I don't know what went wrong," said High Tech. "The computer system is fine. The dam should have released the excess water."

"Instead, the water backed up and flooded the town," said Duke. He turned to Snake Eyes. "Any sign of sabotage?"

Snake Eyes shook his head no.

The team made their way to the overflow station, where two dam workers struggled to open a large hatch.

"Let us help," said Duke.

The four G.I. JOE teammates grabbed the hatch wheel and pulled with all their might. It slowly turned.

SQUEAK!

The hatch sprung open and thousands of rats poured out!

CHAPTER 2

"I've never seen so many rats in one place!" High Tech said with amazement.

The dam workers and the G.I. JOE teammates backed away as the rats scurried down a tunnel.

"They must have clogged the overflow valves," said one of the workers. "No wonder the town flooded."

"What made the rat population explode like this?" asked Heavy Duty.

"I don't know," replied Duke. "Let's ask someone who does."

The four teammates flew the chopper to the local zoo. There they met Dr. Meehan, a naturalist and animal researcher.

"I think I

know the answer," Dr. Meehan said, "but it may lead to an even bigger question."

She took them to the reptile house. They stepped into a room filled with glass tanks holding snakes, lizards, and other reptiles. The snakes squirmed in their cages.

"For several months," said the doctor, "our researchers haven't found any snakes in the wild."

"Snakes eat rats," said Duke, "and if there are no snakes out there, there would be a boom in the rat population."

"That's right," replied Dr. Meehan. "As

you can see, the snakes we *do* have are trying to escape." She pointed to the nearby cages. The snakes inside were slithering against the glass, looking for an exit. "Several have escaped already."

"Escaped?" Heavy Duty asked. He glanced down at his feet — he wasn't a big fan of snakes.

High Tech inspected a nearby tank. The rattlesnake inside rattled its tail and hissed at him. "I have an idea," he said, turning back to Dr. Meehan. "May we borrow one of your snakes?"

"I don't like the sound of this," said Heavy Duty.

CHAPTER

3

Heavy Duty flew the helicopter high above the nearby desert while High Tech studied a computer. On the monitor, a green light flashed, tracking the rattlesnake they had borrowed and released into the wild. High Tech had attached a small transmitter to the snake so they could follow its movements.

"It's still heading west," reported High Tech.

Duke gazed out the cockpit window. "I don't see anything out here but rock and sand," he replied.

"Wait a minute," said Heavy Duty. "What's that, over that ridge?"

Heavy Duty zoomed the helicopter over a large rocky outcropping. It was getting dark, but they could just make out a group of old wooden buildings. They looked like something out of the Wild West.

"It's a ghost town," High Tech said as they flew closer. "People must have mined for gold here, then left after the gold ran out." He glanced down at the computer screen. "Our snake friend is headed straight for it."

Heavy Duty pushed the stick forward. "Hang on," he said. "We're going in!"

Sand swirled around the helicopter as they landed outside of town. The four teammates stepped out and hiked toward the old wooden buildings.

Just as they were about to enter the town, Snake Eyes stopped in his tracks. Duke and the others halted as well.

"What is it, Snake Eyes?" asked Duke.

Snake Eyes looked around and slowly unsheathed his swords.

The sand exploded around them as a dozen strange soldiers sprung from the ground. The soldiers wore COBRA uniforms, but they weren't like any enemy G.I. JOE had seen before.

They weren't completely human.

CHAPTER 4

WHOOSH! Duke ducked as one of the soldiers struck at his head with snake-like speed. Then he jumped as another swiped at his feet with a large scaly claw.

High Tech kicked one of the creatures in its side, but it had no effect. Rows of hard scales ran down both sides of the COBRA soldier's body.

Snake Eyes slashed at one of the beasts with his sword. **CLANK!** The blade merely bounced off its large claw, doing no damage.

The creatures stood like human warriors, but they acted more like vicious reptiles. They were covered with hard scales and let out a bone-chilling hiss before each attack. Yet their giant claws and burrowing abilities made them seem more like sand scorpions — which weren't reptiles at all. The strange combination of animal characteristics didn't make any sense.

Heavy Duty managed to grab one of the deadly creatures. He raised it over his head and hurled it toward four others. The Sand Scorpions went down like bowling pins.

"Come on!" yelled Duke. He dashed for the opening in the enemy ranks. There were too many Sand Scorpions for them to fight at once.

The team sprinted for the helicopter. Four more Sand Scorpions burst from the ground in front of them. The team tried to run around them, but two more erupted from the sand. Then three more!

"These things are buried everywhere!" Heavy Duty said as he punched one of the creatures.

"They must feel our footsteps on the sand," replied Duke, "just like real scorpions!" He spun around and landed a flying kick on another one's midsection.

"Then we better not *run* out of here," said High Tech. He reached into a pouch and removed a small, black box. "Cover me," he said as he extended a long antenna from the box. "I'll fly in the helicopter by remote control!"

Duke, Heavy Duty, and Snake Eyes surrounded High Tech as he moved the small joystick on the remote. The team fought off the increasing number of Sand Scorpions until the helicopter hovered overhead.

High Tech pressed a button and a long rope ladder dropped from above.

Heavy Duty was the first to climb the ladder. He kicked a Sand Scorpion trying to hold him back. Duke was next, followed by Snake Eyes.

Heavy Duty raced into the pilot's seat while Duke leaned out of the open doorway. Snake Eyes stayed near the bottom of the swinging ladder. He reached out an arm toward High Tech.

High Tech grabbed the ladder . . . and a Sand Scorpion's claw clamped onto his leg. He dropped the remote and was reaching for Snake Eyes' arm when another Sand Scorpion grabbed him. And then another! And another!

Snake Eyes strained with all his might to reach High Tech, but it was too late.

The Sand Scorpions carried High Tech away.

CHAPTER 5

Duke watched, clenching his fists angrily, as the Sand Scorpions carried High Tech toward the ghost town. Heavy Duty flew the helicopter higher. Snake Eyes clung to the rope ladder, still reaching his arm out toward High Tech as though frozen in shock.

Heavy Duty buzzed the helicopter over the town. There were Sand Scorpions everywhere. They couldn't land, or they would be no better off then they were before.

Duke glanced at Snake Eyes. The masked warrior motioned for the helicopter to fly lower.

"Heavy Duty!" cried Duke, "get as low as you can!"

Heavy Duty flew the helicopter as low as he dared. Duke looked down the rope ladder, but Snake Eyes was gone. He had disappeared into the darkness.

"Okay, take us back up," ordered Duke.

"If anybody can sneak past those things," said Heavy Duty, "it's Snake Eyes!"

Heavy Duty flew the helicopter back over the ridge.

"Where are you going?" asked Duke.

"I saw something on the way in," replied Heavy Duty. "It may be just what we need."

Once over the ridge, they landed beside the entrance of an old abandoned mine. The two teammates stepped out and ran toward the opening.

"I bet one of these tunnels leads toward that town!" said Heavy Duty.

Duke nodded. "Those Sand Scorpions aren't the only ones who can go underground!"

CHAPTER

6

Silently, Snake Eyes jumped from rooftop to rooftop. Sand Scorpions patrolled the streets below, but they didn't spot him. The ninja didn't know where they had taken High Tech. But he would find his teammate if he had to search the entire town.

Snake Eyes dropped into a dark alley between two buildings. He backed into the shadows as two Sand Scorpions marched by. Hissing loudly, they snapped their giant claws open and shut with each step.

After they had passed, Snake Eyes stepped out of the alley and peered across the street. A dim light shone from one of the buildings. Snake Eyes crept in for a closer look. A faded sign shaped like a large tooth hung above the door. The building must have been a dentist's office. Snake Eyes crouched behind an old barrel and peeked through a broken window.

He saw High Tech strapped to a rusty dentist's chair. His teammate struggled against the leather belts, but he couldn't escape.

Snake Eyes noticed that the walls of the office were lined from floor to ceiling with glass tanks. They contained hundreds of poisonous snakes and scorpions.

So that's where all the snakes went, thought Snake Eyes. *Who in COBRA could be behind such a thing?*

His question was answered when he heard a voice from the next room.

"It's pointless to struggle, High Tech," said the shrill voice. "There's no escape for you now!"

Snake Eyes knew that voice. His suspicions were confirmed when a man in a white coat stepped into his line of sight.

Dr. Mindbender.

"As you can see," the doctor continued, "I've been doing a few experiments with our frightening friends here." He gestured to the wall of snakes and scorpions. "Using their venom, I've combined their DNA with COBRA soldiers to create the fiercest fighting force ever."

Snake Eyes clenched his jaw as he listened to the evil doctor.

"It's a simple recipe, really," continued Dr. Mindbender. He grabbed a test tube containing blue liquid off a rack on a nearby table. "You see, first I extract the reptile DNA." He plucked another test tube from the rack. It contained yellow liquid. "Then I extract the scorpion DNA." He poured the two liquids into a glass beaker. The mixture bubbled slightly and then turned bright green.

Dr. Mindbender closely inspected the steaming beaker. "Now I just need to add the final ingredient," he said with a grin. "That's where you come in." He stepped closer to High Tech. "With my new venom, I will turn you into one of my powerful yet mindless Sand Scorpions!"

The doctor laughed. "You'll have the aggressive power of a snake, the speed and stealth of a scorpion, and the mind of . . . well, a mindless drone!"

"It's not going to happen, Mindbender!" High Tech said defiantly. "The rest of my team will shut you down!"

"I think not," replied the doctor. "I've released hundreds of my Sand Scorpions from their cages. They now patrol this town and the surrounding desert. No one can get past them!"

Almost no one, Snake Eyes thought as he rose and unsheathed his sword. It was time to save his friend.

CRASH!

The barrel behind him exploded into a thousand splinters. Snake Eyes whirled around and came face-to-face with his worst enemy — Storm Shadow! A few slivers of wood fell from the evil ninja's swords.

"I've been waiting a long time for this!" growled Storm Shadow. Swords raised, he pounced on Snake Eyes.

CHAPTER

7

Duke and Heavy Duty ran down the abandoned mine shaft. Heavy Duty gripped a large flashlight while Duke held a small tracking device.

"According to my readouts," said Duke, "we should be getting close to the town."

"Once we're under it, we'll just need to find a way up!" replied Heavy Duty. The two traveled further, then Duke held up a hand.

"Wait a minute," he said. "What's that?"

They both heard a low hum.

"Sounds as if it's just ahead," said Heavy Duty.

As they turned a corner, they saw a strange machine. The device was silver, stood on three legs, and had a large green light that pulsed with every low hum.

"What is that thing?" asked Heavy Duty.

Duke pointed at the ground. "Look out!" he warned.

The two jumped back as a couple of rattlesnakes slithered by. Their tails rattled, but they ignored the two heroes. The snakes slithered to the machine where they coiled into two little piles beneath it.

"That thing must be attracting all the snakes," said Duke.

"But why would COBRA want to do that?" asked Heavy Duty.

"I bet it has something to do with those creatures we fought in the desert," replied Duke.

Heavy Duty aimed the flashlight over Duke's shoulder. "You mean *those* creatures?"

Duke turned to see five Sand Scorpions running up the tunnel. They hissed loudly and their claws snapped open and shut as they closed in.

Immediately, Duke punched one and kicked another. The Sand Scorpions staggered back a few feet but didn't seem to be harmed.

Heavy Duty's solid blows didn't have much effect either. The creatures' heavy scales seemed to deflect any kind of attack.

Duke realized that it wouldn't be long before more of those things showed up. If they could barely hold back five of them, how would they fare against more? Then he glanced at the machine.

"I have an idea," said Duke. "Can you hold them off?"

"I'll see what I can do," replied Heavy Duty. He grabbed a large rock and hurled it toward the creatures.

Duke spun around and examined the machine. Being careful not to disturb the snakes below, he popped open an access panel. He noticed two main cables.

"I can't keep them back much longer!" cried Heavy Duty. He ducked as a giant claw

snapped at his face. Then he kicked one of the Sand Scorpions back into the others.

"Almost there," replied Duke.

He unplugged the two cables and the machine went dead. Then he switched them, plugging them into opposite ports. Once again, the machine began to hum. Duke looked down at the two snakes. They squirmed and quickly slithered away.

Duke smiled. He had succeeded in reversing the polarity of the machine. Instead of attracting scaly creatures, it repelled them!

"I don't know what you did," said Heavy Duty, "but whatever it was, those things don't like it!"

The Sand Scorpions retreated down the tunnel, clutching their heads in pain.

Duke picked up the flashlight and pointed it in the opposite direction. "Now let's find High Tech!"

CHAPTER 8

Dr. Mindbender leaned over High Tech. He held the beaker of venom very close to the G.I. JOE hero's face.

"Don't worry," said Dr. Mindbender, "this won't hurt a bit." He laughed. "Well . . . actually, it's going to hurt a lot."

He tilted the beaker, about to pour the venom into High Tech's mouth.

SMASH!

Snake Eyes and Storm Shadow crashed through the front door!

CLINK! CLANK! CLINK!

Their swords clashed as they madly fought each other.

WHOOSH!

Storm Shadow swiped at Snake Eyes' head. The G.I. JOE ninja flipped backwards and landed beside the wall of snake tanks. Breathing hard, Storm Shadow turned to the doctor.

"I have another specimen for you, Doc," announced Storm Shadow. "Snake Eyes should make an excellent Sand Scorpion."

Snake Eyes raised his sword. He was not going down without a fight. Then the ninja heard something over his shoulder. A snake in a nearby cage was trying to escape. Its tongue flicked as it pushed its head against the top of the tank, lifting the lid.

Snake Eyes looked around the old dentist's office. *All* of the snakes and scorpions were trying to escape. Actually, they were doing more than trying. They *were* escaping!

"What's happening?" asked Dr. Mindbender.

He and Storm Shadow stared in disbelief. Snakes now poured from the tanks and onto the floor.

Snake Eyes leaped onto High Tech's chair. With a swish of his sword, he sliced the straps holding his teammate.

Storm Shadow was about to attack when several rattlesnakes slithered toward him. They wanted out of that room, and he was the only thing blocking their path. Storm Shadow pointed a sword toward Snake Eyes.

"Some other time, Snake Eyes," he said. Then he dashed out the door.

"Wait for me!" cried Dr. Mindbender, racing after him.

High Tech and Snake Eyes crouched on the large dentist's chair. A swirling mass of snakes and scorpions covered the floor.

"Uh . . ." said High Tech, "how are *we* going to get out of here?"

Snake Eyes pointed to the doorway. The snakes and scorpions weren't sticking around. They poured over the threshold like water over a dam.

CHAPTER 9

"Drive faster!" yelled Dr. Mindbender.

The doctor rode in the passenger seat of a transport truck while Storm Shadow drove. They roared down the dusty street toward a large barn at the end of town. Storm Shadow turned sharply several times to keep from hitting crazed Sand Scorpions. The fierce creatures held their heads in pain as they ran into the night.

"We have to get the rest of the venom!" cried Dr. Mindbender.

The truck skidded to a halt in front of the large barn. The COBRA agents scrambled from the truck and sprinted to the entrance. As they swung open the large doors, they were greeted by two unexpected visitors.

"Duke and Heavy Duty!" yelled Storm Shadow.

The two G.I. JOE teammates stood beside a large trap door in the barn floor. Stacks of barrels filled with venom surrounded them.

"I hope you weren't expecting us to help you load this stuff," said Heavy Duty.

Dr. Mindbender staggered back. "No matter," he announced. "I still have the secret formula. I can make as much venom as I want!"

Just then, High Tech and Snake Eyes raced toward them. Storm Shadow placed a hand on his sword. Snake Eyes halted a few feet away.

The ninjas slowly paced toward each other. Everyone watched as the two faced off for an ultimate showdown. Everyone, that is, except Dr. Mindbender. When no one was looking, he climbed into the truck and pulled away.

"You're welcome to stay and fight," said Dr. Mindbender as he drove by, "but I have more venom to create!"

Storm Shadow growled in frustration. "This isn't over, Snake Eyes!" he said as he reached for the passing vehicle. The ninja grabbed the side of the truck and flung himself into the back. He glared at Snake Eyes as the truck drove into the night.

CHAPTER 10

Heavy Duty stared at the barrels of venom. "We have to destroy this stuff," he said.

"I agree," said Duke, "but we should take a sample back to the base."

"Dr. Mindbender said this was an experiment," reported High Tech. "If he uses his venom on more people, we'll need to come up with an *anti*-venom."

"Whoa!" Heavy Duty jumped back as a

rattlesnake slithered by. The rattlesnake wore a small transmitter around its neck.

"Hey, that's our friend from the zoo," said High Tech.

Snake Eyes picked up a rusty container. He scooped up the snake before it knew what happened. He placed a lid on the container and handed it to Heavy Duty.

"Hey! Why do I have to hold the snake?" he asked.

Everyone laughed. It was a well-deserved break from a very long day.

High Tech's smile faded as he stared at the barrels of venom. "If COBRA has the formula to turn man into beast," he said, "what are we going to be up against next time?"

"Whoever it is or whatever it is," replied Duke, "one thing's for sure . . . G.I. JOE will be there to stop them!"

GOOD VS. EVIL: AN EPIC STRUGGLE... AND AN ALL-NEW BATTLE

COBRA® HAS STOLEN THE DNA OF THE EARTH'S MOST SAVAGE CREATURE
TO CREATE AN UNSTOPPABLE ARMY! AND ONLY ONE FORCE ON EARTH
CAN STOP THEM: GI JOE — A REAL AMERICAN HERO®!

A Real American Hero

G.I. JOE

VALOR VS VENOM

DUKE®	AGENT JINX™	SNAKE EYES®	SGT. STALKER™	DUSTY®	COBRA COMMANDER®	ELECTRIC EEL™	COIL CRUSHER™	STORM SHADOW™	OVER KILL™

COLLECT THEM ALL!

GIJOE.COM
for cool new products & more